TIPTOE TIGER

nosy crow

The sun is going down in the jungle,
but Tara is wide awake.

All she wants to do is **bounce** and **pounce!**

There must be time for one last game
before bedtime, but who will want to play?

Look!

Can you see someone over there
with **beautiful, bright wings?**

It's **Butterfly** and her friends!

But will they want to
bounce and **pounce?**

Let's tell Tara to tiptoe up quietly,
just in case they don't.

Whisper, **"Tiptoe, tiger."**

Oh dear. Tara didn't tiptoe.
Her big pounce **frightened**
all the butterflies.

Can you **flutter** your arms
as fast as that?

You can!

But look!
Who's that over there with
the **colourful feathers?**

It's **Peacock!**

Look at all his pretty **colours.**
Which one is your favourite?

Now, we'd better tell Tara
not to scare Peacock.

Whisper, **"Tiptoe, tiger."**

Uh-oh!

Tara **bounced** and **pounced** . . .

and frightened Peacock away.

But look! There's a **tail**
dangling down from a tree.

Can you hold your arms wide
to show how **long** it is?

Who do you think the tail belongs to?

It's **Monkey!**

But we forgot to tell Tara to tiptoe!
And now Monkey is swinging off
through the trees.

It's getting dark now. And **look!**
The owl family have come out
to watch the moon.

How many owls can you **count?**

We'd better tell Tara to tiptoe.

Can you whisper, **"Tiptoe, tiger"**?

Well done. Tara heard us that time!

And can you hear the owls hooting?
Twit twoo! Twit twoo!

Can you **hoot** too?

Oh dear. Tara can't hoot,
but she can roar . . .

Raaaaar!

And **look**,
all the owls are flying away!

I bet you can **roar** just as loudly as Tara.

After all that roaring,
Tara needs a drink.
But who's that lurking in
the middle of the river?

**Look out!
It's Crocodile!**

What should Tara do?

Yes, Tara should tiptoe away
before Crocodile **snap, snap, snaps!**

Can you show Tara how to **tiptoe** away?

Come on, let's say, **"Tiptoe, tiger!"**

You did it!

Tara is **tiptoeing** away
as fast as she can.

But she's not looking where she's going.
Watch out, Tara . . .

It's Tara's **mummy!**
Tara is so happy to be home.
After all that **bouncing** and **pouncing**,
she is feeling sleepy.

All she wants to do now is **cuddle up** with her mummy.

Can you **yawn** like a tired tiger cub?

Yaaawwwn.
And now it's time for bed.

Let's **tiptoe** away and whisper,
"Night, night, little tiger. Sleep tight!"

First published 2021 by Nosy Crow Ltd
The Crow's Nest, 14 Baden Place,
Crosby Row, London SE1 1YW
www.nosycrow.com

ISBN 978 1 78800 653 8 (HB)
ISBN 978 1 78800 939 3 (PB)

Nosy Crow and associated logos are trademarks
and/or registered trademarks of Nosy Crow Ltd

Text © Jane Clarke 2021
Illustrations © Britta Teckentrup 2021

The right of Jane Clarke to be identified as the author
and Britta Teckentrup to be identified as the illustrator
of this work has been asserted.

All rights reserved

This book is sold subject to the condition that it shall not, by way of trade or
otherwise, be lent, hired out or otherwise circulated in any form of binding
or cover other than that in which it is published. No part of this publication
may be reproduced, stored in a retrieval system, or transmitted in any form or
by any means (electronic, mechanical, photocopying, recording or otherwise)
without the prior written permission of Nosy Crow Ltd.

A CIP catalogue record for this book is available
from the British Library.

Printed in China.
Papers used by Nosy Crow are made from
wood grown in sustainable forests.

1 3 5 7 9 8 6 4 2 (HB)
1 3 5 7 9 8 6 4 2 (PB)

To my four granddaughters,
with love – J.C.

To Irina – B.T.